# Peppa Plays Soccer

Published by arrangement with Entertainment One and Ladybird Books, A Penguin Company.

This book is based on the TV series *Peppa Pig*. *Peppa Pig* is created by Neville Astley and Mark Baker.

Peppa Pig © Astley Baker Davies Ltd/Entertainment One UK Ltd 2003.

ISBN 978-1-338-03279-6

10 9 8 7 6 5 4 3 2
Printed in the U.S.A.

16 17 18 19 20
132

First printing 2016
Book design by Angela Jun

**www.peppapig.com**

# SCHOLASTIC INC.

It is a sunny day. Peppa and Suzy Sheep are playing tennis while George watches.

"To you, Suzy!" cheers Peppa, hitting the ball. Now it's Suzy's turn.

"To you, Peppa!" she shouts, hitting the ball straight over Peppa's head. Oh dear!

"Waaaa!" George feels left out.

"Sorry, George," says Peppa. "You can't play tennis. We only have two rackets."

"George can be the ball boy!" cheers Suzy.

"Being a ball boy is a very important job, George," says Peppa.

Peppa and Suzy are having lots of fun, but they keep missing the ball.

"Ball boy!" they shout together.

*Huff, puff!* George is not having fun. He keeps running to get the ball and he is very tired!

Then, more of Peppa's friends arrive.

"Hello, everyone," says Peppa. "We're playing tennis."

"Can we play, too?" asks Danny Dog.

"There aren't enough rackets for everyone," replies Suzy Sheep.

"Let's play soccer, then,"
says Danny Dog.
   "Soccer! Hooray!" everyone
cheers.

"We can play girls against boys," says Peppa.
"Each team needs a goalkeeper," says Danny Dog.
"Me, me!" shouts Pedro Pony.
"Me, me!" cries Rebecca Rabbit.

Pedro Pony and Rebecca Rabbit decide to be the goalkeepers.

"The boys' team will start!" says Danny Dog.

Richard Rabbit gets the ball and runs very fast, right by Peppa Pig, Suzy Sheep, and Candy Cat, and straight up to the . . .

"GOAL!" shout Danny and Pedro together as Richard Rabbit kicks the ball straight past Rebecca Rabbit and into the net.

"The boy is a winner!" cheers Danny Dog.

"That's not fair, we weren't ready," moans Peppa.

Rebecca Rabbit picks up the ball and runs.
"Hey!" shouts Danny Dog. "That's cheating!
You can't hold the ball."

"Yes, I can!" says Rebecca. "I'm the goalkeeper."
Rebecca throws the ball into the goal, straight
past Pedro Pony. "GOAL!" she cheers.

"That goal is not allowed," says Pedro.
"Yes, it is," says Peppa.
"No, it isn't!" barks Danny.
Daddy Pig comes outside to see what all the fuss is about. "What a lot of noise," he snorts. "I'll be the referee. The next team to get a goal wins!"

Richard Rabbit and George run off with the soccer ball while everyone is still talking.

"Where's the ball?" asks Peppa, looking around.

But it's too late! Richard Rabbit kicks the ball straight into the goal, past Pedro Pony.

"Hooray! The boys win!" cries Danny.

"Soccer is a silly game," says Peppa, disappointed.

"Just a moment," says Daddy Pig. "The boys scored in their own goal—that means the girls win!"

"Really?" The girls gasp. "Hooray!"

"Soccer is a great game!" cheers Peppa.

The girls agree!